A Very Haven Christmas

Samantha Baca

Haven Brook Series

'Til Death Do Us Part

The Cradle Will Fall

The Ties That Bind

A Very Haven Christmas

Three Strikes, You're Gone

Cover Design: Oh So Novel

Contents

<u>One</u>

"Oh my," I whispered as he planted kisses down my neck and along my collar bone. It had been so long since a man had touched me and I felt like my body was on fire. My heart raced as my fingers itched to reach out and touch his body. For a man approaching sixty, he had the stamina and finesse of a man in his twenties.

I felt his hand slowly move up to caress my breast under the warmth of my knit sweater. I glanced to the side, checking the time on the clock that sat next to the bed on the nightstand. The kids would be here in less than thirty minutes which meant I needed to get him out of the house before they got here.

"We have to stop, the kids will be here soon for Christmas dinner," I breathed as his body pressed down on mine, the bulge in his pants forcing a whimper to escape from my throat.

"Okay," he breathed as he kept kissing, slowly dipping his tongue beneath the top of my sweater that he had been pulled down low enough to almost show my bra. "But I need to give you my Christmas gift before I go."

"We already exchanged gifts, remember that nice watch I gave you and the beautiful necklace you bought me?" I giggled as he nipped at the lace of my bra.

"Yeah, both of those were great. But I'm about to give you the gift you really want, the gift that neither of us can get enough of." His voice was low and husky, filled with arousal.

I planted my hand against his chest and popped up on my elbows as I looked at him. He stopped, confused as he tried to figure out what happened.

"Wait— you mean to tell me that you're cooking dinner for me today?" I joked as I struggled to keep my face straight. I watched the smile pull across his gorgeous face, up to his golden-brown eyes.

"You know I would in a heartbeat, sweetheart," he said as he leaned forward and kissed my forehead. "But we're not ready for your kids to find out about us yet."

"I know," I sighed as I laid back down and looked up at him. "I'm sorry."

I felt an enormous amount of guilt that I had been hiding my relationship from my kids for three months but there had been so much going on that it never felt like the right time to tell them that I was seeing someone. He was the first person I had dated since their father passed away eleven years ago, and honestly, I never thought I would ever love another man the way I had loved my husband.

"Don't be sorry, it'll happen when the time is right," he assured me as he lifted himself off of me and climbed over to the empty side of the bed. The mood was totally killed and I felt terrible about it.

"I better get going," he said, smiling as he bent down and picked up his jeans from the floor, sliding them up his muscular legs and zipping them as my eyes focused on the bulge that was still there. His chuckle forced my eyes up to look at him. "Don't worry, I'll come back when the coast is clear and we'll finish our gift exchange," he teased.

I stayed in bed for a few minutes, watching him finish dressing as he pulled the t-shirt down over his head, hiding the perfectly sculpted abs that I had run my tongue down not that long ago. This man was far from anything I had ever pictured, even in my wildest fantasies after reading my romance novels. He was pure masculinity with an erotic twist that made me weak in the knees.

A few minutes later I had climbed out of bed and put on the rest of my clothes, giggling when I remembered making love with nothing on but my Christmas sweater. It was a holly jolly good time, to say the least. I stood in front of the mirror as I carefully ran the wand of mascara through my lashes before adding a light peach colored lipstick to counter the flush that was still lingering on my face. I tucked a strand of gray hair behind my ear, debating whether I should make an appointment to get it colored soon? Maybe a light brown color? Take me back to my younger days...

I walked down the hall holding hands with the man who had started to become such an important part of my life. As we reached the front door, I turned to hug him as he wrapped his arms around my waist. I reached up and locked my hands behind his head as I tilted my head to kiss him. His lips were as soft as they were full, and my absolute favorite things to kiss on him. Okay, maybe my second favorite. Within seconds our G-rated kiss had quickly turned into a groping session as we devoured each other's mouths and ran our hands over every body part we could reach. His hands were firmly dug into the flesh of my ass as he kissed my neck when the doorbell rang.

We quickly pulled apart and stared at the door in horror. There was no way that it was already four o'clock, last I checked we still had at least twenty minutes left. I ran my palms down the front of my jeans, wiping away the sweat as I struggled to figure out what to do next.

"Want me to sneak out the back?" he asked quietly, pulling my attention away from the door. I stood staring at him with panic on my face as I thought about what to do. Suddenly the doorbell rang again, sending my heart into a frenzy.

"Mom, is everything okay?" Chase called from the other side before he knocked loudly on the wooden door.

"It's fine," I whispered and shook my head, my hands trembling as I slowly walked forward and turned the lock, counting each second as it passed by. I opened the door and tried to force my face to smile anything other than the terrified, creepy smile that was plastered to it.

"Hey, are you okay?" Chase asked as his brows pulled together while he balanced the newborn car seat on his forearm. I glanced to the side to find Mia watching me with curiosity as she tried to figure out what was going on as well.

"Yeah, I'm fine, I was just in the middle of cooking and didn't expect anyone so soon," I lied. "Come on in, it's freezing out there and I don't want my grandbabies turned into popsicles," I joked as I stepped to the side, panic filling me as I knew what they were about to say. They walked in, Mia first as she held Rylee on her hip with a diaper bag strapped across her shoulder. As they walked in, both of their eyes went wide when they saw that I had company. Chase pulled his head back in confusion before looking at Mia as if she had the answer.

"Lieutenant Dickson, what are you doing here?" Chase asked before looking over at me while he gently set the car seat down next to the couch on the floor. "Is everything okay? Did something happen?"

I felt my cheeks flush as I looked away from my son and glanced at Mia. Her eyes went wide with amusement, her eyebrows nearly shooting off her head when she quickly caught on to what was happening. Buck looked at me, raising his eyebrows as he waited for me to answer.

"Um, Buck is here to check my furnace," I said quickly, looking back and forth between the three of them. I saw the slightest smile pull at his lips as he looked away and ran a hand down the trimmed gray beard that made him look like a sexy silver fox.

"Your furnace?" Chase questioned as he folded his arms across his chest. "Since when does our local law enforcement come out to check furnaces?"

"I was in the neighborhood and your mom mentioned she was having some trouble so I stopped by," Buck said and shrugged as if it was no big deal. "Not to worry, I've checked everything out and she's definitely getting plenty of heat." He turned his head to wink at me, leaning in to give me a quick, friendly hug before saying goodbye to Chase and Mia. The door closed behind him, leaving us in awkward silence.

"I still don't get why you had the Lieutenant come by to check your furnace? You know I would have helped you with it when I got here," Chase said as he tried to make sense of it. I watched as Mia smiled and chuckled before handing Rylee to Chase.

"Don't worry about it, baby. I have a feeling your mom isn't going to have any cold nights from here on out." She laughed as she wrapped her arm in mine and walked with me to the kitchen, glancing over her shoulder at Chase who was still clueless.

Two

"It's not what you think it is," I blurted out as Mia and I walked into the kitchen, keeping my voice low enough so Chase wouldn't hear me. As the oldest of my rowdy boys, he was also the most protective and the one I worried about the most when I thought about how they would take the news of Buck and I dating.

"Why, Connie, I have no idea what you're talking about," Mia chuckled and smiled at me over her shoulder as she reached into the fridge to put away the bottles of milk she had just taken out of the diaper bag. She closed the door and turned around, smiling at me like two girls in the schoolyard who were sharing secrets about their crush.

There was a knock on the front door, followed by Chase getting up to open it. I glanced at the clock on the stove and saw that it was after four, which meant everyone should be showing up around the same time now. I could hear several different voices floating through from the living room and hoped that this would be my saving grace from having to admit what Mia already knew. I forced a quick smile, as I tried to stop the blush that was creeping up my cheeks again before I turned and walked into the living room to greet everyone as they got settled in.

"Merry Christmas my babies!" I squealed as I leaned forward and opened my arms to Liam and Annie as they came running over. I wrapped them in a big hug and kissed the top of their heads before they rushed off to go finish their rounds of hellos. The door opened again and I saw Noah and Jade walk in with Wyatt right behind them. I quickly hugged and said hello to Grant and Lacey before they made their way into the kitchen to put the pies on the table that Lacey had made.

I watched as my family all shuffled about in front of me, holding a hand to my chest as I wished my husband was here to see this. We always talked about how wonderful it would be to watch our boys grow up and start families of their own and how fun it would be to have our house filled with laughter as the kids played on Christmas day. It broke my heart that he never got to see any of this.

Noah and Jade were the last to come in and I was so happy to see them. Noah had been like having a fourth son all these years. He and Chase were inseparable since the day they first met each other. He had always been a part of our family and I was so proud that he was now sharing his family with me. I rubbed my hands together excitedly as Noah unstrapped Asher from his car seat and picked him up, letting him wake up a little before bringing him over to see me. Jade carefully leaned over and kissed his sweet face, gently rubbing her hand across his cheek. I loved watching her with him, the pure love that radiated out of her for her son.

When they first had him, they were so stressed out with finding the perfect name for him. They wanted something that would honor him as their rainbow baby and showed the strength and determination that he had from the start when Jade was told she would likely never be able to conceive. I had suggested Asher after looking up names for them and told them that it was a biblical name meaning miracle or blessing. When they looked at each other, then down at him, I felt my heart skip a beat when they proudly decided to name him Asher.

Jade reached over and stole the baby out of Noah's arms and cradled him against her chest as she walked over and hugged me. I kissed her cheek then looked down at the sweet baby that was trying to fall back asleep against his mama.

"Do you want to hold him?" she asked softly, starting to lift him off of her. I placed a hand over hers and gently patted it, smiling and shaking my head no.

"You let that sweet boy rest, I'll hold him later when he's awake."

She nodded and walked over to the couch, finding a spot in the corner where she could curl up and rest with Asher. I gave Noah a quick hug and a kiss on the cheek as we wished each other a Merry Christmas before he joined Jade on the couch. The room was quickly warming up with all of the bodies buzzing about, so I went over and slid the kitchen window open, allowing the breeze to help cool things off some.

"Why are you opening the window? I thought you were worried about your heater?" Chase asked from across the room, forcing everyone's attention on me. I looked around and saw Mia still laughing in the corner as she tried to hide her face from the others. Wyatt tilted his head and looked at me while Grant looked over at Chase and pulled his brows together.

"What's wrong with mom's heater?" Grant asked Chase.

"I don't know, she didn't tell me anything was wrong with it until we showed up a few minutes early and I found Lieutenant Dickson here, checking on her furnace," Chase said sharply as he looked from Grant then back to me.

"That's funny, I was just here yesterday to fix it. What happened after I left, mom?" Wyatt chided in as he pushed off the wall and folded his arms over his chest, pinning me with a look that said he knew damn well that no one was here fixing my furnace.

"Oh, it was nothing," I waved dismissively in the air. "Everything is fine. Why don't we get started on presents before dinner?" I smiled as big as I could at Liam and Annie, hoping that they would get as excited as I was so we could focus the conversation elsewhere. I watched as Rylee ran around in circles on the carpet in front of the couch, entertaining the kids so they didn't hear me. I scrunched my nose in disappointment when my plan didn't work.

"Okay—now I know something is wrong because mom NEVER lets anyone open gifts before dinner," Grant said as he studied me. I looked around the room at my three *very* protective sons and struggled with how to tell them. I cast a glance over my shoulder to look at Mia, desperate for someone to save me.

"Yeah, and look at how flushed her face is. I don't think she's cold at all. Maybe we should get her to the doctor and have her checked out?" Chase offered as he started a side conversation between Wyatt and Grant.

"Are you sure that you checked the furnace, Wyatt?" Chase asked, getting an immediate dirty look from Wyatt in return.

"Seriously? You are questioning whether I checked the fucking furnace?" He shook his head and glared at Chase. "I'm the only one who comes by to fix things around here and check on her. I think I of *ALL* people know whether the damn furnace isn't working right."

"Well obviously you missed something or Lieutenant Dickson wouldn't have had to go out of his way to come check on it himself," Grant argued and pointed a finger at Wyatt. Lacey walked off to the side and stood next to Mia. She had been in the family long enough to know to get out of the way when the boys started to argue like this.

"Or *maybe* you're all missing something, like the real reason Lieutenant Dickson was at your mom's house on Christmas," Noah said loudly as he raised his eyebrows, everyone's attention shifting to him. He gave me a sly smile that confirmed that he knew what was going on as well.

"Okay, those potatoes are not going to mash themselves," Mia interrupted and walked across the room to stand next to me. "Ladies, let's get in the kitchen and help Connie get dinner going."

I let out the breath I had been holding and gently squeezed Mia's arm as she walked past me, pulling my hand along with her. A few minutes later and I was finally able to breathe as I opened the fridge and stuck my head inside, trying to cool myself off as the blood rushed to my head. Jade and Lacey had joined us and watched me from the table as Mia began working on boiling the water for the potatoes.

"Connie, are you sure you're okay? You look a little overheated," Lacey said as she walked over to the fridge and placed her hand on my shoulder. I could tell that the nurse in her was worried and quickly analyzing whether or not she needed to send me to a doctor.

"I'm fine, dear, thank you."

"She's overheated, alright," Mia giggled from the stove and yelped when I playfully snapped a towel across her butt.

"Mia!" I exclaimed and laughed.

"What?" She pretended to not know what I was talking about. "You know everyone is going to find out sooner than later, and at the rate, the guys are going in there—I would say it's going to be sooner." She lowered her voice as she said it.

"Find out about what?" Jade asked as she sat down at the table and started to breastfeed Asher.

I looked at Mia before looking back at Jade and Lacey, unsure of whether or not to tell them. I knew that everyone was about to find out anyway, and I wanted them to hear it from me, but I had no idea how to tell them that I was seeing someone.

"Umm… well… I… ummm," I stuttered, looking to Mia for help. She nodded and stirred the potatoes once more before setting the spatula on the counter next to the stove and turning to face them.

"Connie had Buck over today to check her furnace because he really knows how to *light her fire* if you know what I mean." She grinned as their mouths dropped in shock as they turned to look at me. I could feel my cheeks blushing again. "Sorry, I can't keep calling him Lieutenant Dickson anymore—not now that I know what's going on," she laughed.

I closed my eyes and covered my face with my hands and I groaned in embarrassment.

"Connie!" Lacey hissed as she giggled from the table. "You naughty, naughty girl," she squealed playfully.

"I can't believe it," Jade said excitedly from the table as Asher continued to nurse. "I'm so excited for you. That might be the best Christmas gift this year."

I lowered my hands and found three beautiful women smiling at me, celebrating the new relationship that I had worked so hard to try to keep hidden because I was scared of what everyone would think.

A VERY HAVEN CHRISTMAS

10

<u>Three</u>

"Alright, dinner is ready," Lacey called to the guys and kids from the kitchen, getting mumbled responses as they stared at the football game on the television. I rolled my eyes and set the bowl of stuffing on the table next to the turkey and yams. Everything looked beautiful and smelled delicious. I silently stood there, watching my beautiful family as I thought about how wonderful it would be to share all of this with Buck. He had been single longer than I had been widowed and I often wondered why he never wanted to find someone and settle down. I knew he had a bad marriage and that his wife left shortly after his son, Jimmy, started getting into trouble, but Buck was a wonderful man and every woman in town knew that.

"Boys- dinner- now!" Mia yelled from the stove, knowing that none of them had bothered coming when Lacey had called them in a few minutes ago. Two six-foot tables had been set up in the small area between the kitchen and living room to fit everyone in one spot while we ate dinner as a family. For so many years I had given up on wanting to have a formal Christmas dinner and allowed everyone to eat off of paper plates and spread out in the living room, eating on the couch and the floor when there wasn't enough room. But this year—this year was different. I was feeling fresh and renewed, and damn it—I wanted a nice dinner where I could sit down and talk with my family.

Jade adjusted the red table cloth that Asher had grabbed and tried to pull off as Mia set up the highchairs in the corner. It felt weird seeing three highchairs around the table when last year there was only one. Our family was growing quickly and it made my heart a little bit fuller with each addition. I took a deep breath and was about to yell out into the living to call them in when I heard them whining and grumbling about an interference and how 'the ref must be drunk if he didn't see that' as they came into the kitchen and scattered around the table to take their seats.

Once everyone was situated, I did a quick check to make sure we had everything we needed on the table and sat down in the only empty seat, which happened to be the head of the table. I felt my chest tighten as I recalled Christmas dinners when the boys were younger and their father sat at the head of the table. I swallowed hard, busying myself with picking up my napkin and laying it on my lap. The room was quiet overall as everyone focused on passing the dishes around, serving themselves and each other, until everyone's plates were full.

I waited a few seconds, unsure of whether to say grace since we hadn't done that in years. Chase smiled at me as he reached his hands out, taking Mia's on one side, and Lacey's on the other, before bowing his head. Quickly everyone followed his lead and the room was silent as they bowed their heads. I cleared my throat before saying a quick prayer, thanking the Lord for our meal as well as the time we were spending together as a family. As I finished, I sent up a silent prayer that he would help guide me on how to come clean about why Buck was here earlier.

Forks clanked against the plates as they started to eat. I busied myself with cutting my turkey into small pieces, feeling the nervousness bubble up inside of me.

"So, how was everyone's Christmas morning?" I asked, trying to stall as I started a random conversation.

Chase and Mia mumbled *good* as they focused on feeding their girls. Rylee wanted to be a big girl and do everything herself since she was going to be two in a few weeks. Millie was just excited to sit in her highchair and smear mashed potatoes across the top of it, stopping every now and then to lick some off of her hands.

"It was good, I got a baby for Christmas," Annie said proudly as she sat up taller in her chair and took a bite of turkey.

"How exciting, what is your new doll's name?" I asked in between bites. From the corner of my eye, I could see Grant and Lacey exchange nervous looks as they shifted in their seats.

"It doesn't have a name yet, but I'm hoping that one is a boy, and the other is a girl."

"Two babies, wow, that's really exciting! You must have been a good girl to get TWO babies," I said happily.

"I guess." She shrugged her shoulders and pushed her turkey around her plate with her fork as Liam leaned in and whispered something in her ear. Something was going on but I couldn't figure out what. I turned to look at Grant and Lacey who now had a deer caught in the headlights look on her face.

"Something is going on, what is it?" I asked as I narrowed my eyes at my middle child. He was always the first to crack under pressure and I knew he would come clean if I pushed hard enough.

"Actually," he said as he set his fork down on his plate and looked around the table before turning his attention back to me. "Lacey was the good girl. She's pregnant."

I let my fork fall from my hand as I covered my mouth and squealed in excitement. Everyone started talking, offering their congratulations.

"Are you sure she was a good girl?" Wyatt joked, glancing at me from the corner of his eye knowing that I would get on him for being rowdy around the kids. "Seems like maybe she was riding the naughty list when that happened."

I felt the laughter bubble up inside me and tried to hold in before I failed miserably. I burst into laughter at his joke and snorted, causing the room to go into hysterics.

"Mom, what has gotten into you today?" Grant joked playfully as he tapped my arm with his elbow. "You're feeling a little rowdy."

"I think maybe your mom has been riding the naughty list too," Noah teased, ducking as Chase threw a bread roll at his head.

"Shut up, my mom isn't seeing anyone," Chase said defensively before looking over at me. "Tell him, mom."

I tried to keep a straight face as everyone's eyes were on me. Without warning, I burst into another fit of laughter as I tried to think of a more tactful way to say that I had indeed been riding the naughty list.

"Okay, since it's going to come out sooner or later, I might as well just get this over with," I said with a heavy sigh once I was able to stop laughing. I glanced at the kids, making sure they weren't listening before I continued. "Buck—Lieutenant Dickson—and I have been... *working on my furnace* for a few months now." I decided to word it carefully when I saw Liam look up and started to listen.

Noah brought his fist to his mouth and tried to hide the laughter as his head rolled back and his chest shook. Jade elbowed him to get him to stop as she laughed and smiled at me. I looked over to Chase, Grant, and Wyatt, trying to gauge their reaction to the news.

Chase stared off into the distance, looking as if I just told him that someone shot down Santa's sleigh and he didn't make it. Grant worked his jaw back and forth as his foot tapped on the floor next to me. And Wyatt looked at me with a huge smile on his face as he shook his head. I raised my eyebrows to silently ask him why he was smiling.

"I fucking knew it," he laughed and slapped the table. "There was no way that anything was wrong with your furnace."

"Language!" I scolded as I looked pointedly next to him at Liam and Annie. He rolled his eyes and smirked as he started laughing again.

"Nope, your mom has definitely had something warming her up this winter," Lacey joked, earning a quick glare from Grant.

Chase stayed silent at the other end of the table, looking upset.

"Are you okay?" I asked, making sure to raise my voice enough to grab his attention so he would know that I was talking to him. He waited a few minutes and just stared at me.

"I just can't believe it…" His voice trailed off as his words lingered in the air. I felt my heart sink, knowing that he would be the one who would have the hardest time with me dating someone.

"Honey, I'm sor—" I started before he looked directly at me and cut me off.

"His name is *Buck?*" He wrinkled his nose and frowned.

"That's what bothers you?" I asked as I tilted my head to the side in concern.

"Yeah, I guess I just never knew him as anything other than Lieutenant Dickson. It feels so weird to hear you call him *Buck*."

"I'm sure that's not all she calls him," Noah quipped as he ducked to avoid another bread roll, this time from Grant. Everyone laughed and suddenly I felt more relaxed about coming clean and having everyone know my little secret.

"So, are you guys okay with this? I know that I haven't dated anyone since your dad passed," I asked sincerely. I was excited to see where things could go with Buck but at the same time, there was no way that I could continue on with him if one of my kids wasn't fully on board with it. Their happiness has always been the most important thing to me and I wasn't about to change that now.

"We're okay with it, mom, really," Chase said as he looked around the table at his brothers before his eyes locked onto mine. "We just want you to be happy. And if *Buck* makes you happy, then we're happy."

"Are you seriously going to keep saying his name like that?" Wyatt leaned forward to look at Chase.

"What?! I might be happy that mom found someone to make her happy and that she enjoys spending time with—but I will always know him as Lieutenant Dickson- the guy that caught me smoking pot outside of the school and turned me in."

"At least he didn't catch you having sex," Grant said as he nodded across the table at Wyatt who had a faint blush creeping up his cheeks.

"I don't think you want to start sharing dirty secrets, big brother," Wyatt responded and glanced at Lacey's hand. Suddenly everyone turned their attention to her as she desperately tried to pull her hand under the table to hide it.

"Son?" I asked and nodded to Lacey. He pursed his lips and glared at Wyatt before looking around the table.

"Well, I guess since we're all sharing with each other, Lacey and I have more news to share with you guys."

"Besides her being pregnant?" Chase asked, obviously having missed Wyatt's nod at Lacey a few seconds ago.

"Are you ready to tell them?" Grant asked Lacey who was almost as white as a sheet of paper. She nodded her head yes and slowly pulled her hand up from under the table.

"Lacey and I got engaged this morning," Grant announced proudly as she held her hand up for everyone to see the ring that sparkled in the light. "And, not only is she eight weeks pregnant, but we're having twins."

I jumped up out of my seat and waited for him to stand up as I wrapped my arms around him and hugged him. This was turning out to be one of the best Christmases we had had in a long time.

<u>Four</u>

After dinner, I sent everyone into the living room to hang out and watch the rest of the football game while I worked on the dishes. There was so much energy flowing through me that I needed to be up and moving to get rid of it. I scraped the last plate clean, watching as the few bites of food fell into the overly full trash can. I set the plate in the sink on top of the others and turned to open the pantry to get a new trash bag when I bumped into Wyatt. I clutched my chest as my heart began to race.

"Wyatt! What are you doing there? You scared me half to death," I exclaimed, trying to calm myself.

"Sorry, I didn't mean to scare you. I thought you heard me behind you," he laughed as he opened the pantry and pulled out a trash bag. He slid the trashcan over with his foot so it was out of my reach as he took the full one out and put the new one in. He grabbed the heavy bag and carried it outside to the trash for me. I was at the sink, rinsing the dishes when he came back in.

"Here, let me help you," he offered, gently pushing his hip into mine to scoot me out of the way.

"You don't have to help clean up, you should go watch the game with your brothers."

"Eh, my team is losing anyways," he smiled and began filling the sink with hot water to wash the dishes that couldn't go in the dishwasher. "Plus, you did the cooking, you shouldn't have to do all of the cleaning too."

"Well thank you," I said, proud of how he turned out to be such a sweet and caring man, just like his father was. "But don't tell the others that I let you help me, I forced them out of here and wouldn't let them help me even though they insisted."

"It'll be our little secret," he winked and turned off the water before picking up the sponge to start washing the dishes. I felt myself blush when he said *secret*, wondering if he had known all along that I was seeing someone. He had reacted differently than the others, almost as if he knew.

"It seems there were a lot of secrets revealed today," I said, hoping to lead into the conversation that I really wanted to have with him. One thing about Wyatt was he didn't talk about things if he didn't want to, and I honestly didn't know if this was something he would want to talk about.

"Yeah, there sure were," he answered as he scrubbed the plate and rinsed it. I took a slow, deep breath in and held it for five seconds, releasing it just as slowly.

"How do you feel about everything that came out today?" I knew that he would know where I was going with this conversation and prayed that he wasn't going to force me to just come out and ask him about it.

"I think it's great that Grant and Lacey are getting married and having babies. It's like a big baby factory around here lately," he chuckled and smiled at me.

"Ain't that the truth?" I laughed and finished loading the dishwasher before turning it on. My head was still spinning when I thought about how next Christmas there would be seven grandbabies running around my house. I was so excited, I could hardly stand it.

"But that's not what I'm talking about and I think you know that," I said gently as I stood next to him, my back against the counter so I could look at him while he washed the dishes. He sighed and dropped the sponge, letting it sink into the water as he pulled his hands out and rinsed them before drying them on the towel hanging next to the sink.

"I'm happy for you mom," he said as he turned around and leaned against the counter, facing the same direction as I was. "As long as you're happy, that's all that matters to me."

"Did you know that I was seeing someone?" I asked quietly, not sure that I wanted to know the truth. He nodded but didn't say anything.

"How long have you known?" I looked up at him.

"For a few months," he shrugged and kept staring straight ahead of him.

"How did you find out?" I asked, suddenly worried when he looked nervous and his shoulders tensed.

"It doesn't matter," he said nonchalantly.

"Wyatt…"

He leaned his head back and exhaled heavily before turning to look at me.

"I came by one night to check your actual furnace and didn't know you had company. I thought maybe you were out with your friends when you didn't answer, so I used my key and let myself in. Once I heard you in the bedroom, I left and vowed never to come over unexpectedly again after that." He arched an eyebrow as he watched the color drain from my face.

"So let me get this straight—my boyfriend once caught you having sex, and now you've caught me having sex with the same guy who caught you?" I asked, embarrassed as I processed that new piece of information and added it to the collection of things that I couldn't ever un-know.

"Yup." He made a popping sound with his lips.

"Let's agree to never talk about this again? Ever?" I asked and extended my hand for him to shake. "Not even with your brothers." I raised an eyebrow as I extended my hand further. He laughed and shook my hand as he agreed.

He turned around and went back to the dishes while I grabbed a washcloth and started wiping down the counters.

"So, how are you feeling? Are you still doing your therapy?" I pressed, knowing that he didn't like to talk about it.

"Na, I gave up on that."

"Why? I thought you said they thought it would help?"

He stopped what he was doing and clenched his jaw, the anger evident on his face.

"I know that you don't want to talk about it, but I really think you should."

"I don't need to talk about anything, mom," he snapped, forcing me to flinch at his tone.

"I'm sorry," he apologized softly. "I just hate talking about it."

"I know."

He lowered his head and let out a sigh as the weight of everything that had happened this year sat heavily on his shoulders.

"It's not fair. That's what I hate the most about it. I had a scholarship that I can't do anything with now because the doctors won't clear me to play again because my heart is too fragile," he said sarcastically.

"Wyatt, you were stabbed several times in the chest. You lost a lot of blood. The doctors had to work very hard to keep you alive because your *fragile* heart kept giving up," I said firmly as I reached over and placed an arm around his shoulders. Or at least tried to. He was almost a foot taller than me so it was a hard reach. "I know that it breaks your heart that you can't play baseball anymore, and I know that it sucks. But I thank the Lord every single day for giving you back to me because it's not always that easy. Very few people are given a second chance at life, but you got one."

I gently squeezed his shoulders and felt some of the tension slip away.

"You know, I would do it all again in a heartbeat," he said matter-of-factly.

"What's that dear?"

"Being stabbed and almost dying. I would go through all of that all over again to save Lacey." He gazed over the half-wall that divided the living room and the kitchen. I followed his gaze to where Lacey was sitting on the couch, curled up next to Grant, holding hands as they watched tv by the fire.

"I would never want that, none of us would. But I know that we all appreciate how selfless you were when you sacrificed everything to save her. Especially your brother."

"Well, she's a special girl who deserves to be saved. And my brother needed someone like her in his life, especially after everything he's already been through. He and Liam both."

I blinked to try to clear the tears from my eyes as I thought about sweet Renee and how she was taken too early, forcing Grant to raise their son on his own. I knew the pain of losing a spouse and being left to care for children as a single parent but I never thought my own son would have to experience it at such a young age. When no one else could reach Grant as his life spiraled out of control, Wyatt stepped in and was the one who had saved him from himself. They've had an unbreakable bond ever since.

"Someday you're gonna find a woman just as special, and you'll be adding to the baby factory yourself," I teased, watching as his face scrunched up.

"No way, there's not a girl out there who can settle me down. Not any time soon, anyway," he joked and went back to washing the dishes.

22

<u>Five</u>

The night slowly went by as we sat around entertaining each other with sharing funny stories while indulging in pie and drinking hot chocolate. My heart felt fuller than it had in a very long time and part of me wondered if it was because my family was growing or if it was because I had finally allowed someone new into it. For the longest time, I swore that I would never love another man, that my heart would forever be closed off to finding new love, because I had made that promise on my wedding day. But the more that I allowed myself to step back and really look at things, I found that I wasn't trying to replace the love that still held a huge piece of my heart. I was simply allowing the love to grow in a place of my heart that I never knew was there.

I glanced down at my watch to check the time, knowing that it was getting late and everyone would be heading home soon so that the grandkids could wind down and rest for the night. I was also starting to feel giddy about calling Buck to let him know that I had finally told my family about our relationship so we no longer had to hide it. This also meant that I didn't have to get creative with ways to hide his vehicle every time he came over. It was seven-thirty when I heard the doorbell ring, puzzled as to who it could be when everyone I knew was already here.

I got up and walked over to the door, looking over my shoulder as I felt Chase's eyes on me. He smiled and looked away, planting a kiss on Millie's head as he bounced her on his knee. I turned the knob and opened the door, surprised to find Buck standing on the other side with a bottle of wine. My reaction must have startled him because he suddenly looked panicked and looked past me to where everyone was hanging out in the living room.

"What are you doing here?" I whispered as I leaned in so no one else could hear me. "I thought we said we would talk later after the kids were gone?"

He opened his mouth to speak but stopped and looked over my shoulder.

"I called him and asked him to come join us," Chase whispered loudly, mimicking me over my shoulder. I tilted my head upward to look at him, surprised that he would do something like this.

"You called him and invited him over?" I asked as I continued to think through this. He nodded his head yes and extended his hand out to Buck.

"I'm really glad you could join us tonight, Buck, please come in if my mom will pick up her jaw and scoot out of the way," Chase teased as Buck shook his hand.

"Thank you for inviting me, it's a pleasure to be here," Buck laughed and handed me the bottle of wine as he wrapped his arm around my waist and leaned in to whisper in my ear, "I'm guessing they know?"

"Mmhmm," I murmured and stepped to the side to let him come in. "It's been a very revealing Christmas with plenty of sharing to go around."

He arched a brow and looked at me, sending a shiver through me as I took in how good looking he was. His short black hair with streaks of gray was freshly trimmed, and it looked like he had shaved since this morning as well. I took a deep breath and inhaled the spicy scent of his aftershave, anxious to rip his navy button-down shirt off of him and strip him of the dark denim jeans that perfectly hugged his ass. I cleared my throat and tried to force the thoughts out of my head as I closed the door and led him into the living room.

"Everyone, I would like you to meet Buck," I said nervously as they all turned their attention to us. "I know you all know him as Lieutenant Dickson, but now that you are aware of our relationship, I would like you to call him Buck and treat him as the special friend that he is to me."

I felt relieved when they all took turns saying hello and coming over to welcome him. I would never have imagined that I would be able to spend Christmas with my kids and my new boyfriend—was he actually my boyfriend??—at the same time. The thought that we were all here together at the same time was blowing my mind.

We found a space on the floor by the fire and sat down to join everyone as they talked about their plans for New Year's Eve. I was sitting next to Buck as he wrapped an arm around my shoulders casually and leaned in close to me.

"Do you have plans for New Year's Eve?" he whispered in my ear. I shook my head no. "Good, because I was hoping that you would join me at my house and I could make dinner for you for a change."

"That sounds wonderful, I would love to." I turned to face him and gently cupped his cheek in my hand, debating on whether it would be inappropriate to kiss him. The kids knew about our relationship, but that didn't mean that they were ready to see us together yet.

"When do you start your new job?" Grant asked Wyatt, pulling my attention away from Buck.

"After New Years'," Wyatt responded, looking nervously at me.

"What new job?" I asked, wondering why he hadn't told me about it. Wyatt and I were probably the closest out of all of my kids, and last I knew he used to tell me everything. He looked down to avoid meeting my eyes as he pulled at a loose thread on the pillow next to him.

"I just accepted a new job as a Recruiting Coordinator for the Haven Brook University baseball program. I'll be scouting new talent across the state, and on occasion, I might have to go out of state. But right now it will be a lot of travel, that's why I was waiting to tell you."

I felt my body tense as he told me, my fears that he would completely abandon his dream of playing baseball again finally being true. I knew that he was having a hard time being patient with his recovery after the stabbing and the numerous surgeries he had to undergo, but I also knew how important it was for him to keep playing. Baseball has always been important to him, ever since he was a little boy and his dad coached his little league team.

"Is this what you really want?"

"It is. I've thought long and hard about it and while I would love to keep playing baseball, I don't think it's going to happen for me. That's why I stopped doing physical therapy. They might hope that someday I'll get to where I can play again, but I know deep down that it's likely over for me. This job allows me to still be a part of it, without having to worry about my own recovery."

I nodded my head and felt Buck gently squeeze my shoulders as he stayed silent. Everyone's attention was focused on our conversation while the kids were off in Liam's room playing.

"If you're happy then I'm happy. That's all I ever want for you. For all of you," I said as I looked around the room and smiled.

"Thanks, mom. I thought you were going to be upset about it," he admitted sheepishly.

"Why would I be upset?" I asked.

"Because I gave up on my childhood dream, I let go of the one thing that I still shared with dad. It's like I let go of him." His voice cut off and I could hear the pain in his words.

"Son, you are more than baseball. You always have been. We've been passionate about it because you loved it so much but we've never wanted you to feel like we would ever love you any less if you didn't keep playing. Your dad would be proud of who you are, regardless of whether you kept playing."

He gave me a tight smile and went back to picking at the loose thread.

"So, do you have any prospects lined up yet?" Buck asked, jumping into the conversation.

"Yeah, I'm actually checking out this kid who is really good in East—" he paused and looked at Lacey with panic on his face.

"Easterville," she finished for him and smiled sadly. "We have a lot of good talent there, I can ask my cousin Kayce if she knows anything about the prospect you're checking out since she still lives there."

"Thanks, but that's okay. I want to slide into town without anyone knowing why I'm there. I think that's how you really learn about someone."

"Don't lie, you just want to sneak around and check out the local girls before you have to do your actual job," Noah teased.

Everyone started laughing and the rest of the night flowed easily from there. Soon, everyone was saying goodnight and heading home. I waved to Grant and Lacey from the door as they packed the kids into his truck and drove off. As I shut the door, I realized that Buck was still there and we finally had the house all to ourselves.

"So, about that Christmas gift you were wanting to give to me this morning…" I teased as I hooked my finger into his belt loop and pulled him down the hall to my bedroom.

Six

I rolled over and snuggled up to Buck, feeling happy and content to be waking up in his arms and not having to worry about him sneaking out before the neighbors saw him there so word didn't get back to the kids. Now that the kids all knew about it, I didn't care about who in town knew and were gossiping. They could say whatever they wanted to at this point, nothing would ruin this new happiness that I had found.

Gently, I ran my fingers along his chest, tracing circles as he slowly started to wake up. I scooted closer and kissed his cheek, whispering good morning in his ear.

"Good morning," he drawled out, still half asleep.

I laid my head on his chest and closed my eyes, still feeling tired from our marathon love making last night. We'll just say that he gives the *best* Christmas gifts and I planned on staying on the naughty list for next year. We stayed snuggled up together for a little while longer and, for once, neither of us worried about the time. I knew that Liam and Annie were coming over later to spend the day with me but we still had hours before they would be here.

"What are your plans today?" he asked sleepily as he rubbed my back.

"I don't have any until later this afternoon, Liam and Annie are coming over for a bit so Lacey and Grant can celebrate their engagement. I'm having the kids sleepover so they have the entire night, though I'm not sure how long Lacey will stay awake," I giggled, hearing Buck chuckle along with me. I had given him the updates on everyone last night after they had all left and excitedly told him that I was going to be a nana again in July and that Lacey was expecting twins.

It felt wonderful to share the news with Buck and feel his excitement along with mine. Things started to feel like they had shifted between us, that we had a stronger connection now that we weren't trying to hide our relationship anymore. Once I saw how genuinely excited he was to hear about all of the things happening in my kids' lives, it made the wall around my heart crack a little bit more, allowing him in.

"Sounds like fun," he said as he looked down and smiled at me. I returned the smile but could swear that I saw a hint of sadness on his face. "I'll be sure to head out before they get here."

When I heard his words, I knew what the problem was. Even though we had made a lot of strides in our relationship in the last twenty-four hours, it was still so fresh that he was having a hard time feeling like he was part of my family.

"What are your plans today?" I asked, leading into my formal invite.

"I don't have any, other than going to visit Jimmy at some point this weekend."

"How is he doing?" I knew that he didn't like to talk much about his son and the trouble he was constantly in because everyone in town judged him for what Jimmy did. If Jimmy was caught with drugs again, it was Buck's fault for not keeping an eye on him as a child when he first started experimenting. If Jimmy robbed a store, it was Buck's fault for not knowing where he was at all times so he could protect the people of the town since he was the Lieutenant. It was really unfair and I hated that he constantly felt the weight of his son's actions.

"He's good, I guess. Staying out of trouble for the most part."

"Well, that's as good as anyone could ask for," I joked, feeling his chest rumble as he laughed.

"If you don't have any plans *today,* maybe you could stay and we could have a pizza and movie night with Liam and Annie?" I felt my voice crack a little as I asked it.

He pulled back and I could feel his eyes on me. I slowly pulled my head back and looked at him. There was a serious look on his face and I immediately started to wonder if it was too soon to be inviting him into all of my family stuff.

"You don't have to if you don't want to, it's not a big deal," I said hurriedly, trying to move past the awkward moment.

"You really want me to be here with you and the kids?" He tilted his head to the side and watched me.

"I do," I nodded. "Buck, I would love nothing more than to have you be part of my family and share everything with me. It's not about spending the holidays together, it's about sharing everything with each other. And I want you to be in my life for a very long time, which means that I would love for you to be here for pizza and a movie night with the kids."

I watched as tears flooded his eyes as he quickly tried to blink them away. Buck and I had talked several times when we first started dating about how hard it was to find someone who would fit so perfectly in the life we had created. For him, it was hard to find someone who understood that no matter how many times his son messes up, he will always love him and be there for him because he is his son. He regretted that he never found another woman to love and that he would likely never have grandchildren that he would know about. For me, it was hard to want to let someone into my life when I finally had things the way that I wanted them and I worried that they would undo everything that I had worked so hard to create.

"I would be honored to be a part of the pizza and a movie night," he whispered as he leaned in and kissed me.

"Okay," I laughed, "But it's going to be at least three movies and none of us can ever agree on one pizza so we end up with at least two different pizzas, the kids split theirs in half with their own toppings. I get the special."

"Well, I just happen to love the special and I would stay through four movies." He winked, making my heart flutter as I leaned forward and wrapped my arms around his neck before giving him the biggest kiss ever.

30

<u>Seven</u>

It was after two when Grant and Lacey showed up to drop the kids off and I was starting to feel a little anxious about springing it on them that Buck would be hanging out with us tonight. I knew that this was a big change for everyone and prayed that they would be okay with it so that I didn't have to break Buck's heart and cancel on him after all.

I opened the door and smiled as Liam and Annie came running up the driveway with their overnight bags strapped to their backs. They rushed up and wrapped their arms around me. I loved the brother-sister bond they had formed so early on, thankful that Liam finally had the sibling he had always wanted. My heart nearly burst when I found out that they were both going to get to share the experience of having two new siblings in seven months. I let go as the kids ran off and went inside, saying hi to Buck and dropping their bags by the door. Grant and Lacey were a few minutes behind them, smiling as they came up the driveway.

We said a quick hello then went inside to get out of the cold. I waited with bated breath for them to say something about Buck being there but instead I was pleasantly surprised when Grant went over and gave him a quick hug, followed by Lacey. Everyone seemed happy and I started to feel silly for stressing about everything in the first place. Perhaps I had been worried for so long about how it would impact other people if I met someone who made me happy, that it made it hard to accept that I felt this way.

"You look beautiful, Lacey," I said as I went over and sat on the couch next to Buck. The kids were already back in Liam's room, getting their stuff situated and picking which movies they wanted to watch from the list I had made this morning. I tried to make things as fun as I could when they would come over, so today I decided to pretend they were going to dinner and a movie at the theater. I left a menu for them to order their pizza and a list of different movies that would be showing tonight. Buck helped me make tickets for them to use for popcorn and candy that they could 'purchase' at the concession stand.

I don't know who was more excited about it—Buck or the kids. We ran out to the store this morning to grab a few things and ended up coming back with a bag filled with the movie theater-sized boxes of assorted candies, a 12 pack box of popcorn, and a variety of popcorn seasonings. When I gave in and agreed to let Buck get the stuff to make root beer floats, I couldn't stop smiling when I saw how excited he was. It felt wonderful to let him be part of this and to do things with the grandkids he never expected to have on his own but has always wanted.

"Thank you," Lacey said with a quick blush on her cheeks. "Grant and I are going to dinner in Eastern Point tonight and getting a room at the hotel I've been dying to stay in. We figured we might as well enjoy a romantic, kid-free night before I get too pregnant to be able to enjoy it." She laughed and leaned into Grant's shoulder. He wrapped his arm around her and planted a kiss on her forehead.

"We do want to talk to you about something real quick before we go," Grant said, his tone changing the mood in the room. I felt my stomach knot as I dreaded what he was about to say.

"I can leave so you guys can talk," Buck said quietly, patting my knee before standing up.

"You don't have to do that," Grant interrupted. "I think it would be best if you stayed for this."

Buck hesitated for a minute before looking down at me and sitting down. Grant blew out a quick breath and glanced at Lacey before turning his attention back to us.

"Alright, here it goes," he paused and looked at Lacey again, getting an eye roll from her in return. She reached over and playfully swatted at his chest, laughing at how dramatic he was being.

"Just get on with it and tell them, or I will. These babies are getting hungry and you promised me a snack before dinner," she teased. I laughed and was thankful that Lacey's mood was still the light and playful one she had since she came in, hoping that their 'news' wasn't as bad as Grant was making it out to be.

"Okay, Lacey and I have set a date for our wedding," he blurted out as a huge grin spread across his face. "February 14th."

I took a minute to let it sink in, knowing that Lacey and I had talked a while back about how hard it was to date after being widowed, and she had mentioned that she didn't want to rush into getting married again. She wanted a long engagement to make sure that it was the right thing to do before she made that type of commitment again. I felt her eyes lock onto mine and knew that she recognized the puzzled look on my face. She smiled softly as if she knew what I was thinking, remembering our conversation herself.

"When we settled everything with Derek's estate, I found that there were a few boxes that I had left in Montana after we rushed to move in with my dad. I was in such a frenzy as the grief took over me that I had completely forgotten about them. My best friend agreed to ship them to me, and when I opened them, I found my mom's wedding dress." She sighed heavily and took a deep breath before continuing. "I struggled with what to do with it, but in the end, I decided that I wanted to honor my mother by wearing it at my wedding. I didn't have anything that she left to me, nothing that was a part of her. And while the dress felt tainted at first because it was the dress she wore when she married my dad, I decided that I didn't have to look at it that way. When she married him, she thought she was marrying the man of her dreams. She was ready to make those vows to the man that she thought the world of."

She stopped and looked up at Grant as a tear slid down her face.

"And I want to do the same. I love this man so much that I couldn't imagine living a second of my life without him. I don't want to slow down and risk missing out on a minute of happiness."

Grant reached over and gently wiped away the tears that were flowing down her face as he pulled her closer into the side of him and hugged her.

"I think it's a wonderful way to honor your mother, dear." I felt my own tears threatening to spill out of my eyes as Buck reached over and squeezed my hand.

"We know that it's a very quick engagement, but we were hoping that maybe you guys could help us with some of the planning since it's less than two months away and you both have some connections in town." Grant looked between Buck and me as we sat in stunned silence.

"You want me to help?" Buck asked quietly.

"We would be honored if you would," Lacey chimed in with a smile. "After all, you are a very important part of the wedding party now that you're family."

"Thank you, Lacey, but I think you have the wrong idea," Buck started and I could feel his body tense against mine. Lacey's face fell and her shoulders slumped as she waited for him to speak. "I'm the one who would be honored."

I felt the tension in the room evaporate as quickly as it had mounted.

"Well, it looks like we have a lot to do in a short period of time," I joked, confirming that I was fully on board to help them with whatever they needed. "Not that I'm not excited about the wedding coming so quickly, but what made you guys decide to get married on Valentine's Day?"

"My mother was four months pregnant with me when she got married, and I'll be right around four months with the twins at that time. I just pray that I can still fit in her dress with *TWO* babies instead of one."

The room was filled with laughter as we joked and teased each other for a few minutes before they left for their date. Liam and Annie were still in their rooms, arguing over which movie to watch first. I curled up on the couch next to Buck and tucked my feet under me as he wrapped a blanket around me and let me snuggle against him.

"Well, this Christmas has been a whirlwind of changes with everything happening so fast," I said as I listened to his heart beat beneath my head. "I still can't believe that they're getting married in less than two months," I chuckled.

"I'm really honored to be a part of everything," he said quietly. "I know we've talked plenty of times about how we wanted to take things slow and how hard it is to allow someone into your life after so long. If things are starting to move too fast, or if I'm getting too much into your space—please tell me and I'll gladly back off some."

I shifted my position so I could look up and see him better.

"Buck, there's nowhere else I would ever want you to be. I thought that this would be a hard thing to do, but it turns out that it's really easy to open up and share your life with someone when you've found the right person."

His face lit up as he smiled. I wasn't sure when he was happier- now that I'd confessed my feelings for him, or earlier when he was loading our shopping cart to the top with junk food for the kids tonight. Either way, I was glad that not only did I get to be a part of it but that I was the reason for it. It turned out that once you started letting the walls down on your heart, it was easy to want to take them away completely when you found someone that fit so easily into the empty space you never thought you could fill.

A VERY HAVEN CHRISTMAS

Eight

The days seemed to fly by after Christmas and before I knew it, it was already New Year's Eve. I had spent time with each of the kids throughout the week, each of them having their own plans for New Year's. Buck had stayed with me almost every night, only going home for short periods to change his clothes and take care of a few things. It felt so weird that we went from sneaking around and hiding our relationship a week ago to having him practically live with me. I enjoyed his company so I didn't complain other than when he had to leave.

Tonight, Buck had invited me over to his house for dinner and I was feeling anxious like a teenage girl who was expecting her first kiss. I had no idea why I was so nervous, it wasn't like we hadn't slept together already. The thought of him cooking me dinner and having me go to his house felt like we were taking our relationship to a whole different level when it forced me out of the comfort and safety of my house. When we were together at my place, I felt like I was in control of almost everything. Now he was in control and I was feeling completely out of sorts.

I glanced in the mirror one last time before deciding to put on my pearl necklace that would go great with the black lace dress I was wearing. It was sleeveless which made me feel self-conscious, but Mia and Jade had assured me that I looked sexy when they stopped by earlier to help me get ready. They were both so sweet and caring to come over and walk me through a handful of wardrobe options as they told me how stunning I looked in almost everything that I tried on. It felt like I was young again, getting ready for a date with my best girlfriends by my side to help me.

Mia loaned me a pair of black strappy shoes that had a four-inch heel that I was terrified would trip me and I would break my neck before we even had dinner. She assured me that I would get used to them in no time and Jade confirmed that they made my legs look even longer and sexier with the dress that hit my legs mid-thigh. My fingers trembled as I clasped the necklace in place and rubbed my lips together, watching as the red lipstick vanished then reappeared. I took one final deep breath before picking up my cell phone from the nightstand and stuffing it into my purse before heading out the door to Buck's.

Ten minutes later I was walking up to his door, legs shaking as I started to doubt my ability to walk in these heels without making a complete ass out of myself. I knocked on the door and waited. Finally, I heard whistling as he got closer and opened the door. He had a towel slung over his shoulder, the smell from inside floating out around me and making my stomach growl. He stepped back to let me inside as his eyes traveled up and down my body.

"The food smells delicious," I said as I leaned in and kissed him. His hand slid down my waist and cupped my ass as he leaned in and kissed me back.

"You *look* delicious," he replied with a sexy smile. I looked down at myself nervously, pulling my lip in between my teeth.

"Thank you."

"Dinner is almost ready, why don't you come in and I'll pour you a glass of wine?"

He closed the door behind me and turned to walk back to the kitchen, extending his hand out for me to take it as I followed him inside. I had only been inside his house a few times but it reminded me so much of my parent's house from when I was a little girl. Suddenly, I felt the calmness take over as I walked with him through the living room to the kitchen that was attached. I loved that his house was wide open and wished that mine was bigger and had the space he had. I would love to be able to cook in the kitchen while my family hung out in the living room, laughing and talking, and I could still be a part of it.

I sat on the barstool he pulled out for me at the island that separated the two rooms. The island was huge and had four cushioned stools that slid under it so they weren't in the way. I loved that there was hardly any clutter in his kitchen, everything having its own place. He opened the wine and poured two glasses, extending one to me before taking a sip out of his glass. He set it down and walked to the stove behind him to check on the food that was cooking.

I slowly sipped my wine as I watched him move about the kitchen, admiring his abilities to move so easily without spilling anything or burning himself. He looked at ease with every movement and I wondered if he had been an actual chef at some point. My eyes gazed on his nicely sculpted body as the button-down shirt he was wearing pulled tight across his shoulders when he bent down to pull a pan out of the oven. He was wearing the same jeans he had worn over to my house on Christmas—the ones that really showed off what a great ass he had.

Ten minutes later, he led me to the table in the dining room that had a beautiful bouquet of red roses in the middle with a cream-colored tablecloth underneath. He had taken the time to set the table, including a bottle of champagne that was chilling in a bucket of ice beside the roses. I brought a hand to my chest and gasped at how beautiful everything was as he smiled proudly. I took my seat and allowed him to serve me, feeling like a pampered princess as he waited on me.

Dinner was delicious and I made a mental note to wear baggy clothes the next time I let him cook for me. After we finished, I offered to help with the dishes but he shook his head no and led me to the living room where he started a fire and laid out a blanket on the floor in front of the fireplace. He ran off to the kitchen as I got situated on the floor and brought back the bottle of champagne and our glasses. I grabbed a few pillows from the couch behind us as he sat down to join me.

I kicked off the heels that I had been wearing and tossed them to the side while he situated the pillows behind us. When I turned around I found him on one knee in front of the fire, holding out a black box with a red ribbon on top.

"I know it's not Christmas, but I have one more gift I would like to give you," he said nervously. I watched anxiously as he slowly opened the box, showing me a beautiful diamond ring.

"Connie, I know that we haven't been dating long and we both agreed to take things slow, but I thought long and hard about what Lacey said the other day about not wanting to miss a single second of happiness. You make me happier than anyone I've ever known and I don't want to miss a single second of happiness with you either." He stopped and pulled the ring out of the box, his fingers trembling as he held it out to me. "Would you do me the honor of being my wife and making me the happiest man in the world?"

I felt my heart skip a beat as I looked back and forth between the ring and the man who had stolen my heart.

"Yes," I said breathlessly as I extended my hand and watched as he slid the ring onto my finger. What I expected to be a moment of doubt and sadness ended up being a moment of absolute certainty as I kissed the man that I was excited to spend the rest of my life with.

<u>Nine</u>

Buck and I rang in the new year cuddled up by the fireplace, drinking champagne, and making love. I was blissfully satisfied with how my year ended and even more excited about how the new one was starting. There had been so much that had changed in my family over the past few years that it felt weird for the change to finally be with me. We agreed to sleep in and start the first day of the new year on the right foot—fully rested and in each other's arms. I rolled over and cuddled into him, feeling the roughness of his beard as it tickled my face when he leaned in to kiss my neck. I wrapped my arms around him and giggled.

"Good morning," he mumbled against my shoulder.

"Good morning, *fiancé*," I whispered back to him, feeling on top of the world.

"I love the sound of that." He leaned forward and kissed me softly.

"Me too," I said, meaning every word. I ran my fingers up along his shoulder then down his back, making lazy circles.

"When did you want to start telling the kids?"

I froze for a second, the first time I had thought about having to tell them. I wasn't worried that they would be upset about it given how quickly they had warmed up to him already, but I did wonder if they would feel like it was too soon. For me and Buck it didn't feel rushed at all given that we had already been dating for a few months but for the kids, it might feel like it happened in the blink of an eye since they barely found out a week ago.

"I don't know," I said nervously. "I want to tell them right away but…"

"But you're scared that they'll think we're moving too fast," Buck finished my sentence for me. I nodded and slowly pulled in a deep breath, hoping it would help relax me.

"I understand your apprehension and if you want to wait a little while before we tell anyone, that's fine with me."

His words soothed me better than any calming breaths could. That was one of the things that I loved the most about him was that he knew me so well, he could tell when I was stressed or upset about something, and he was able to easily defuse the situation before it overwhelmed me.

"I'll tell them soon, I promise," I assured him with a smile. "There's just a lot going on right now with Wyatt starting a new job on Monday, Grant and Lacey rushing to plan a wedding, and Chase and Mia getting ready for Rylee's birthday next week—it's so much at once and I don't want to add to anyone's stress right now."

"It's okay, Connie, really." He reached over and gently ran the pad of his thumb across my cheek.

"Thank you, I appreciate your support."

"Well, you better get used to it because you're going to marry me and from what I've heard—that's what married folk are supposed to do," he joked, lightening the mood between us.

We spent the rest of the day together, putzing around the house while talking about random things in between the meals he cooked. I was definitely going to take him up on any future offers to cook from here on out. I found that he could make even the most basic things—like grilled cheese and tomato soup from a can—taste like it was made in some gourmet restaurant. After lunch, we cuddled up together on the couch to watch a movie but I couldn't help but notice how tense and nervous Buck was suddenly acting. Every few minutes he would check his watch or his phone, keeping an eye on the time instead of paying attention to the movie.

"Is everything okay?" I pulled away and looked up at him so I could read his expression. I was a mom of three rowdy boys so I knew how to easily read when someone was lying to me.

"Yeah, I'm fine," he said nervously, avoiding my eyes and focusing on the tv. Liar. I folded my arms across my chest and continued to glare at him until he turned to look at me. I waited as he squirmed in his seat, adjusting his position anxiously.

"Buck…" I warned with the same tone that usually worked with the boys.

He slightly turned his head to look at me, a forced smile on his face that looked almost painful.

"What is going on?" I demanded, my irritation growing the longer he avoided me.

"Nothing, let's watch the movie." He patted my thigh a few times and looked back at the tv as if he had any idea what the movie was about. Then, when he thought I wasn't looking, he looked down at his watch again.

"Okay, that's it," I said as I stood up and threw my hands in the air. I knew that all of this was a big change for him as much as it was for me, but if we were going to make this relationship work, he needed to be honest with me and tell me that he wanted some time to himself. Maybe it was a little too soon to get engaged?

I reached down and picked up my cell phone from the coffee table and shoved it into the pocket of the sweatpants he had loaned me so I didn't have to wear my dress all day. I debated changing back into it so I could give him back the clothes he let me wear but I was too angry and frustrated to care about it right now. I would go home, fix something for dinner, and toss them in with the load of laundry that was still waiting for me from a few days ago.

"Where are you going?" he asked as if he had no idea why I was so upset. This infuriated me even more.

"I'm leaving, Buck. I'm going home and giving you your own space so you don't have to check your watch and phone every few minutes. If you wanted me to leave, you should have just said so," I bit out angrily.

"I don't want my own space, Connie. You know that. I wouldn't have asked you to marry me if I did," he explained with a stern tone.

"Then why have you been sitting here watching the time for the last hour? Something else has clearly had your attention and I don't want to be the thing that is keeping you from whatever it is that you'd rather be doing." I put my hands on my hips and waited for him to respond.

"Why don't we get out of the house for a few, get some fresh air? Maybe we can head back to your place and spend some time there?" he suggested with the grin I couldn't resist. I eyed him suspiciously, wondering what he was up to. "I'll even cook you dinner…"

I laughed and rolled my eyes. Had I been reading the whole thing wrong? Maybe he wasn't wanting me to leave so he could do something else—maybe he was feeling restless from being at home for so long and he really did need to get out and get some fresh air. We did spend a lot of time at my house so it would make sense that he would want to go there and hang out for the rest of the night. I let out a sigh and felt calmer as he guided me out the door and to his truck.

A few minutes later, we pulled into my driveway and I felt the comfort of being home again. He reached over the console and gave my hand a quick squeeze before we got out and walked up to the door. I unlocked the door and walked inside, holding the door open for Buck to follow. When I turned the corner to go into the living room I felt my heart jump out of my chest as everyone screamed 'surprise' and threw confetti in the air toward us. My eyes quickly scanned the room, finding that all of my kids and their families were there, smiling while they waited for me to process what was going on.

I felt Buck's hand on my lower back before he leaned down and chuckled in my ear.

"Surprise," he said playfully.

"What in the world… what is all of this?" I asked, watching as Chase and Grant came over to shake Buck's hand while the girls came over to hug me.

"Congratulations! We're so excited for you!" Lacey squealed and held my hands.

I looked up at Buck who was grinning from ear to ear, soaking up the excited energy that was flowing through the room.

"Did you plan this?" I asked him as everyone started to quiet down some to listen.

"I didn't plan this, no. But, I did tell the boys that I was going to propose before I did it. I wanted to get their permission beforehand and they were all very supportive of it. They were excited for us and asked if they could tell the ladies and before I knew it, a surprise engagement party was being planned," he laughed, spreading his arms out.

"This is amazing, thank you guys so much!" I brought my hands up to my cheeks and looked around the room at the beautiful family that was the symbol of what love is.

I made my way around the room getting hugs from everyone and showing off the ring. The kids had put everything together for us, including order pizza for dinner so no one had to cook or clean up. We laughed and talked for hours, my heart feeling fuller than it's ever felt. Soon everyone was packing up and heading home to get ready for the new week. I was standing at the door, waving goodbye to Chase and Mia when I saw Wyatt lingering in the hallway.

"Are you heading out too?" I asked, noticing the look of concern on his face.

"Yeah, here in a few."

"Is everything okay?" I reached over and gently squeezed his hand.

"I'm not sure about taking that new job tomorrow," he said nervously.

"Do you want to come sit down and we can talk about it?" I asked, nodding to the couch. Grant and Lacey were still packing up their things while Liam and Annie went through the stuff in their room that they needed to take home. He looked over at them then shrugged his shoulders as he made his way over to the couch. I followed his lead and sat down beside him.

I waited a few minutes to let him start the conversation but when he sat there in silence, gently rocking back and forth, I decided to take charge.

"What happened with the job? Why are you reconsidering?" I asked gently, grabbing Grant's attention as he turned toward us.

Wyatt looked up at Grant then over to Lacey before blowing out a heavy sigh.

"I don't know, something just doesn't feel right. I can't explain it but it feels like if I take this job, something bad is going to happen."

"Do you think maybe you're just nervous because it's a different type of job than you've had before?" I kept my tone soft to make sure he knew that I wasn't judging him or trying to tell him how he should feel. Honestly, I was worried about him taking this job as well but for different reasons. I hated the idea of him having to travel so much for work because it meant that I wouldn't know where he was most of the time or if he was okay. Buck had already laughed and thought I was borderline crazy when I asked if we could sneak a GPS tracking device onto his car so I could know where he was at all times. Then Buck reminded me that I probably didn't want to know where he was at *all* times.

"I guess it could be nerves," he sighed. "But it feels like if I take this job then I'm admitting that this is what I am. This is all that I'll ever be. I will have officially given up on trying to pursue a baseball career of my own. What if I'm giving up on myself too soon?" His voice rose slightly, the desperation and fear creeping up with it.

I reached over and held his hand again, finally understanding what was bothering him. I was struggling to find the words to say when Grant came over and kneeled in front of him. He arched an eyebrow and waited until Wyatt looked at him.

"What have I always told you?" Grant asked as he stayed at eye level with Wyatt.

"You've told me a lot of shit—some of it helpful, some of it not," Wyatt joked until Grant gave him a pointed look. "Fine," he sighed dramatically. "You have always told me that I'm whatever I want to be."

"Exactly," Grant replied. "And taking this job does not mean that you're giving up on yourself. It means that you value and respect yourself enough to go after new challenges. Your body is healing and trying to recover. You can't force it to do what you want it to do, Wyatt. That's not the way it works. If and when you heal the way you need to, baseball will still be waiting for you. If not, then you remember it as a wonderful part of your past and your work your ass off to create the future you want."

I leaned back against the couch and watched my two sons, the bond between them stronger than I could have ever prayed for. It made me happy to know that they loved and would always be there for each other. Wyatt sat in silence for a few minutes, processing Grant's words.

"Is there anything we can do to help you with the stress you're feeling with taking the new job?" I asked.

"Na, I think that helped," he said with a smile. "I just need to get out there, try something new, and see what the future holds for me. Who knows, maybe it will be good to get out of Haven Brook and see what else is out there."

"Yeah right, you just want to get out there and see what *girls* are out there," Grant joked, clapping him on his back as he stood up and walked over to Lacey.

"Well, you found Lacey and she's a catch… just saying, there might be more to Easterville than this kid I'm supposed to scout." He winked at Grant who had wrapped an arm around Lacey's shoulders and scowled at him.

"Trust me, you don't want to mess with the girls in Easterville," Lacey laughed. "They're all a little bit crazy. Except for me, I was one of the good ones."

"What about Kayce?" Grant asked, looking down at her. "Is she one of the good ones or one of the crazy ones? Just so I know how deep the crazy runs in that side of the family before these babies get here," he joked as he rubbed a hand along her stomach.

"Oooh, Kayce is a good one but she is also crazy. She's equal parts." She giggled and wrapped her hand over Grant's.

"Maybe I'll have to find her and say hi while I'm out there," Wyatt teased with a wink, back to his usual self.

"Oh sweetie, that girl is a man-eater. She will eat you alive," Lacey warned playfully.

Buck walked over and sat next to me on the couch, joining in on the conversation as we laughed and teased Wyatt about his rowdy ways. He wrapped an arm around me and snuggled me close as he whispered, "I really love this family."

"So do I, and that includes you," I said before I tilted my head up and kissed him.

A VERY HAVEN CHRISTMAS

<u>Other Books By Samantha Baca</u>

<u>The Haven Brook Series:</u>
'Til Death Do Us Part (Haven Brook Book 1)
https://books2read.com/u/m2RJNR

The Cradle Will Fall (Haven Brook Book 2)
https://books2read.com/u/b6O0QE

The Ties That Bind (Haven Brook Book 3)
https://books2read.com/u/mqgoz8

A Very Haven Christmas (Haven Brook Book 4- Novella)
https://books2read.com/u/mvqGjj

Three Strikes, You're Gone (Haven Brook Book 5)
https://books2read.com/u/mvqL2z

<u>The Dark Shadows Series</u>
Five Steps Ahead (Dark Shadows Book 1)
https://books2read.com/u/38Q0gO

Ten Seconds Too Late (Dark Shadows Book 2)
Coming 2022

Against The Clock (Dark Shadows Book 3)
Coming 2022

Out Of Time (Dark Shadows Book 4)
Coming 2023

<u>The Stone Creek Series (Novellas)</u>
Chocolate Covered Mistletoe (Stone Creek Book 1)
https://books2read.com/u/3LRk9N

Candy Coated Promises (Stone Creek Book 2)
https://books2read.com/u/mldP5Y

Pumpkin Spiced Possibilities (Stone Creek Book 3)
https://books2read.com/u/bojdwV

<u>Stand-Alone Books</u>
One Last Wish
https://books2read.com/u/mqg7D9

Finding Love In Apartment 2C (Novella)
https://books2read.com/u/bze9aZ

Acknowledgments

There are certain things that bring you those warm feelings that make you feel good inside, like holidays spent with your loved ones, or really good books. I hope that Connie's story brought you a little bit of both. I've enjoyed writing the Haven Brook series and I have fallen so deeply in love with these characters. I love this world and desperately wish it really existed because it would be a cool place to live with a wonderful group of people.

Thank you to everyone who has read this short, sweet holiday novella. I hope that it pulled at your heartstrings every now and then as we watch this family grow. Not to worry, Wyatt will be getting his book next.

I would like to express my sincerest gratitude and appreciation to my very loyal alpha readers, Chelsea and Azucena. They read every single book that I write and have fallen in love with these characters the same way that I have. Your excitement and reactions to the books as I write them is what keeps me motivated to make these the best they can be. Thank you both for constantly being there for me and making these books so easy to fall in love with.

Thank you, Tillie, for being such a fantastic help with the editing and proofreading, as well as assisting with the plot. I don't always look forward to the edits because of the errors I've made (haha! Just kidding) but I do look forward to all of your notes that you leave me about the book. I find myself laughing at them when no one is around. But if no one is around, am I still crazy?!

Richard, you are and will always be my number one supporter and the only person who makes sure each book gets done quickly, and correctly. Thank you for taking my passion and helping me uncover it. I wouldn't do half the things I do if it wasn't for you. I love you more than any of the characters in these books and you know how much I love them. You're my real life love of my life and I simply adore you.

I would like to say a giant THANK YOU to all of my friends and family who continue to support me and recommend me to their friends and family. I see every social media share and I appreciate every review. You guys are the best!

As always, I'm thankful for the love and support of my parents and sister. They constantly remind me that the sky is endless and to never stop reaching for the stars. Even if I've collected a few, there are still plenty more that are waiting for me.

To my sweet girls— thank you for still taking naps every now and then so mommy can write. I love you both more than you'll ever know and I hope some day you look back on the things I've accomplished when you were little and that it makes you proud.

To all of the readers, if you've read this far, you're definitely on my favorites list! Thank you so much for spending your time reading my books. If you've enjoyed them, I ask that you might consider jumping over to Amazon and leaving a review. It would mean the world to me and I would forever be grateful.

About the Author

Samantha lives in the southwest with her husband and two small children after abandoning her childhood dream of living in a cabin in Colorado when she found that she couldn't afford to live there and was deathly allergic to the woods. When she's not writing she's usually spouting off sarcastic remarks while drinking wine out of a coffee mug to look like a functional adult while chasing down her toddlers. She enjoys spending time with her family, watching reruns of FRIENDS, and the 24/7 flow of coffee that can be found in her veins. Be sure to follow her on social media for updates on what she's working on.

You can find her here:

Facebook: https://www.facebook.com/AuthorSamanthaBaca

Instagram: https://instagram.com/author_samantha_baca

Goodreads: http://www.goodreads.com/authorsamanthabaca

Facebook Reader Group:
https://www.facebook.com/groups/2945710968775398/

Webpage: https://authorsamanthabaca.wordpress.com

Newsletter: http://eepurl.com/g0NcSj